DUST IN THE WIND

JOSEPH WAMBUA

ISBN: 9789966190413

DEDICATION

To all our loved ones who have left this world for the next. You are always in our hearts. Nobody can replace you. We loved you then, we love you now and we trust we shall join you some day to love you even more.

CONTENTS

MONDAY

2ND AUGUST 2004

1 MONTE KLINIKUM HOSPITAL, FORTALEZA, BRAZIL.

9.55 a.m.

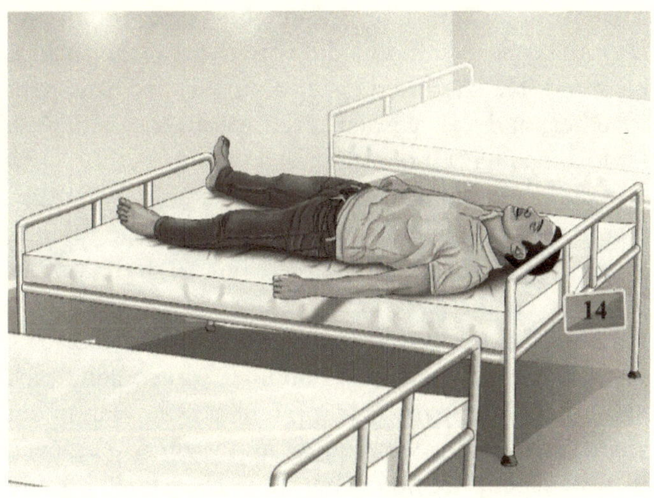

A pale yet imposing figure lay motionless on a bed
labelled fourteen. His eyes were barely open but many

others around him were inadvertently drawn to him. The curious eyes saw a body that was filled with all the traces of strength and good health but all that seemed to be running out of its time. The little they could read from his confused glare was more of psychological rather than physical pain. He probably knew something no one else did and it was definitely eating him slowly, but surely. Whatever it was, it couldn't have been good or the least bit pleasant. His breath didn't elicit lots of promise, if any. Something was going very wrong and the battle he was fighting appeared to be increasingly becoming futile.

Staring into a large resounding emptiness, he seemed to be fighting more than one battle. There was a world out there which he loved so much especially so, his family. Edvaldo knew so well, as sure as the sky above that they loved him back equally. He had never imagined living without them. They were his life. They meant the world to him and everything he ever did he did with them at the back of his mind. He cherished every moment they had spent together and he wished each could be renewed. Unfortunately, that could not be.

Like the Amazon River travelling downstream where it had no choice but to empty into the Atlantic Ocean, he too had no choice but to taste calmer waters. There had been many happy moments together. Those moments challenged each other to a flashback in his exhausted mind. He too couldn't pick any to lend a particular preference. Any moment shared with family was equally important to him even if it was spent fighting. They were all marvellous and uniquely memorable.

All through, his family had always been there to

share his ups and downs but right now, he felt so alone. This one, they just couldn't share. Even if they formed an army all around him, they couldn't fend off the enemy ahead. This was one fight, he had to battle alone. The only weapon he had left was his characteristically strong will, which was also failing. All his other guns were down and out and this last one was proving to be difficult even to hold. Suddenly, his mind was all made up.

A fight was lost.

2 KISII, KENYA.

11.15 a.m.

Up above in the sky, there were massive clouds that wore a dark grey colour. They didn't look like they could hold the millions of water drops that composed them any longer. Miles below the clouds, Kerubo stood for a moment gazing up at them, maybe trying to solve the puzzle of the sudden darkness that had befallen the earth. For a brief moment, her face took on a disturbed look but she didn't allow it to last. The sky with all its might wasn't going to interrupt her. She looked back down and the goal she had embarked on early in the morning became clearer than before.

With a single swipe, she rid her forehead off a load of sweat. Another bead broke immediately after, just as a chilly wind rushed by. She went back to digging the thirteenth hole that day.

She needed them to plant bananas to feed her family.

The first drops of rain fell heavily on her. They soaked her tattered clothes that were very much reminiscent of those worn by slaves in the southern territories of America back in the eighteenth century. She dug on completely ignoring the rain. Her home was just a few meters away so if it got really bad, she could quickly run to the house. Besides, she hated leaving anything half done.

Intermittent flashes of light from the sky interrupted the darkness that had casually set in. The sky also vented out its wrath in a deafening roar of thunder. Still, Kerubo lifted up her hoe each time promising herself it was the final time.

The earth she painfully earned a living from was red, full of fertility and iron as well. She stood firmly on it. Crystal clear waters from heaven had washed off all the sweat but she stood her ground, determined to leave that hole ready for hosting a banana plant.

The rain started pounding more vigorously. There was a lot of anger up above and Kerubo wondered if it was directed at her or someone else. It became apparent that she couldn't accomplish her little mission. She dropped the hoe and made a leap towards the house but the sky was already too furious.

A web of electricity lit up the sky much brighter than before, stopping Kerubo at her second leap.

3 ROOM 013 HOTEL NA`RODNY` DOM, BANSKA` BYSTRICA, SLOVAKIA.

4:31 p.m.

Two figures lay in a compromising position without a care, zestfully searching for comfort, warmth and unbridled intimacy. There was lots of satiation emanating from them. Both lay without shame in the state that Adam and Eve were after consuming the forbidden fruit. They themselves had had quite a bit of the forbidden stuff.

Alisa slipped out of the five star comfort of the bed. She was stark naked – she couldn't look more beautiful. Nudity had nothing to do with it. The woman was quite a looker no matter how she was displayed. Nothing had been overlooked during her creation. A pair of eyes apprehended her sight lusciously. They had been savouring that nudity for many moments, yet they seemingly hadn't had enough of it.

Only two people had a right to view her in that precious state. One was definitely watching. After all, he was omnipresent but the eyes currently cherishing in that sight certainly didn't belong to the second rightful person. This Eve didn't belong to the Adam she had been lying next to, let alone unreservedly displaying her delicacies to. This Eve belonged to another and so did this Adam.

She made a couple of steps with a lot of character widely aware of the lust filled eyes trailing her. "Quit devouring me with your eyes."

"And why not? I haven't had enough of you yet."

Alisa let out a striking giggle. "Thanks for the complement my dear but you can do with just a bit of me for once."

Shooting out of the bed and stopping right in front of her, "A bit of you!" He exclaimed taking his hands round her waist. "I don't think so." He made the thoughts in his mind and the wishes of his body very clear.

"Don't be greedy" she said with a very unconvincing straight look. He started to respond but she stopped him with a hand over his mouth. "Ssh! Ondrej, I have to go. I have an important meeting."

"With whom?" He attempted to play down her reason for refusing to heed to his self-gratifying though evil call.

"Hey! There are so many people I could meet.

Like my husband, my children…"

His grip round her waist tightened. "With whom?" He demanded to know certainly not amused by the cat and mouse game she was trying to play.

With some unexpected disgust at his persistence and without thinking carefully about what she was about to let out of her mouth, she answered, "With God." Then she tried to wriggle out of his grip but it was a bit too tight. "Let me go Ondrej." Her voice was soft while airing lots of calm and yet very uncompromising.

The way she said these last words implored his better judgment to take charge and let her loose. His tongue though was quick to ruin it all. Breathing heavily in her face he said, "I'm your boss, remember?"

"How can I ever forget that?" She asked with rage strongly built into her voice. She hated to be reminded of that and she found it to be a stupid and weak form of intimidation. It was time he found something else other than her job to use as bait. She thought it very lame of him to use her job to blackmail her into sinking more and more into sin.

"Then I'm telling you not to go now."

"Hey!" She started with a little smile. Actually, his persistence gave her a sense of pride. She felt very important and special. "If you spend all your energy with me what will you do with your wife?"

"Unless you want to be there to witness it, don't ask." "Fine, I won't ask but I have to leave now."

"No, you don't."

"Yes, I do." She retorted trying to make her way around him but he took a step to stand in her way. "I have a very important meeting Ondrej."

"If you say so but if you leave, consider yourself fired."

It was difficult for Alisa to spare Ondrej a laugh in his face. "Fired from what, the job or from sleeping with you?"

"The job of course."

She chuckled. "Sorry but you fire me from one, you fire me from both." Much more than before, she felt decidedly obliged to leave.

She really would have wanted to stay on and enjoy the stolen moment but there was a call at church. It was a Wednesday and like every other Wednesday and Saturday, she went for choir practice. Yeah! She was a dedicated choir member who sang devotedly at church every Sunday.

Wednesday's practice session was usually short, lasting only an hour from 6pm. For some other reason, she liked getting there earlier. In fact, she always got there earlier than everyone else. This time she wasn't so much early, just twenty-five minutes before time. For a brief but tantalizing moment, she stood at the church's main entrance a little hesitant to go in. That's not where the practice was usually held. There was a hall reserved for that purpose.

Something was persistently pushing her in while another was pulling her away. Some inner voice was telling her it's the wrong time to do it but what could be wrong with saying a little prayer. Besides, she had a heap of sins to confess to. She even smelled of one.

She took a couple of strides in and sat herself at the end of the second last pew. Her palms went over her face as she closed her eyes to pray. Her prayer however didn't start with the forgiveness part. There were thanks to give and by the time she was halfway, someone else was seated close by.

That was the good old shepherd. Well into his fifties, he wore his traditional grey suit and black shirt with the white collar. He was dressed for the job but right now, he sat next to Alisa who had just come from work. She wasn't exactly appropriately dressed for a meeting with God. Seated on that pew, her dress a little shorter than should've been, Pastor Domino yearningly looked down at her legs.

Alisa felt a hand touch her skin, not on her hands but on her thighs. She didn't seem disturbed about it. Even though her eyes were closed, she had identified the owner of the hand. Soon the hand got bolder and adventurous, seeking to discover the rest of her legs.

Her prayer started dragging, slowly losing the words to say to God. Soon the adventurous hand went further up completely drying out words from her mind. She started revelling in the sensations the hand was causing her. The prayer stopped but her eyes remained closed. She had not yet reached the forgiveness part.

The Pastor lived in the church compound with his family of five. His wife was just in the house waiting for her husband to call but he was calling elsewhere. She was always ready to be submissive like her husband kept preaching to his congregation but at this moment, he wasn't there to be submissive to. He was in his office preparing his next riveting sermon. As a good wife, she never interfered with his noble work of gathering and nurturing good flock for the Lord.

Pastor Domino had conducted an affair with Alisa from his office for a while now. Sure, that office behind the pulpit he so well preached from. One would have thought that's the place the Holy Spirit came down to fill him with God's message for his people. The heavens had grown too restless. They had a lot of wrath to rent out and the time had come.

The last natural disaster seismologists expected in the city was an earthquake. Tremors here and there didn't mean much. They could never be devastating– or so they thought.

Then suddenly one came. First Alisa and her seatmate felt the earth move a little. It didn't stop them from enjoying their moment but that was just a warning, may be to test if they could realize their wrongs. They didn't. How could they when it felt so wonderful? Like Lot's wife during the destruction of Sodom and Gomorrah, they went on and did what they had been warned not to. Well, even Noah did warn the whole world but none listened. These were just two souls.

A second tremor followed seconds later, wild and unforgiving. God was very angry. How could they use his house to commit such evil acts? His wrath suddenly went out of control and the ground below the couple opened up instantly swallowing up the couple. The church was split into two. A deep rift sunk harrowingly between it. That horrifying crack on earth didn't extend far from the church. Other parts of the city only experienced the earthquake.

Alisa and Pastor Domino were gone. God had even spared their families the trouble of burying them. But gone also was the lovely church built through the sweat and efforts of many dedicated Christians. Did the heavens have to destroy a house of God just to punish two souls? The answer wasn't far off. It was right there in the holy book. For a new house free of any sins, it was necessary.

4 PATTAYA-CHON BURI, THAILAND.

6.34 p.m.

The sun had travelled to the west faster than usual.
It sped as though it was in a hurry to get somewhere.
Day was fast turning into night. Six-year-old Nissa
suddenly realized it was way past his predetermined

time for getting into the house. Without a word to his friends, he abandoned the football game and dashed off. Trouble was the last thing he wanted but even as his little feet rushed him home, he wasn't sure he could make the line in stipulated time.

It was already too late. The welcome he received wasn't the one he had prayed for but the one he had anticipated and greatly dreaded. His stepfather was already home and the look on his face wasn't a pleasant one. Nissa didn't remember it ever being pleasant anyway. He knew he was in trouble but just how much was anyone's guess. The moment he stepped into the house he found his stepfather already on his feet, which wasn't a good sign. Mom certainly wasn't home.

Nissa placed his bet on shutting his eyes to what his eyes could see so clearly. He decided to run past the tower of trouble and make his way to the bedroom where he could lock himself until his only saviour got home. He didn't make it past his stepfather. The man he called dad stopped him in his tracks with a hard kick on his side. It sent him flying only to land heavily on the floor. Dad had worn the face of the devil and done it so well. To prove that he too could take command in the absence of Satan, he followed him down on the floor, picked him up and knocked his head against the wall really hard. Then as if the boy was something really disgusting to hold, he let him drop down like a piece of filth.

"Where were you this late you idiot?" He bellowed.

The boy sat there quietly. He didn't shed a single tear and didn't move a muscle either. With little signs of life, his eyes kept to his dad accusingly but that didn't rid him of the devil entrenched deep inside him. Ten minutes later he still sat there staring into space. For a moment his stepfather thought he was dead. Just to ascertain his suspicion, he stealthily walked closer. Unlike before, this time he was afraid of touching him. "Oh thank God!" He relaxed when he heard a whisper of life in the boy's faint breath.

Nissa's mother walked in from work sending a sudden chill through her husband's spine. She could always read him like a book and not necessarily a very interesting one at times like this. The moment she looked at his face she knew that something wasn't right with her son. Nothing had been right with her child from the day she walked into that marriage. Her husband's face told her that whatever it was, he had everything to do with it.

"What is it Akkharat?" Sinee impatiently asked her husband.

"I…I don't know. Maybe you can tell me," he played with words thinking they could help his situation.

She wasn't in the least bit convinced. His act was so poor any fool could see right through it. One glance in Akkharat's direction and there he was. Her only son, the only thing she had to show for much of her life on earth was halfway on the cold floor and halfway against the wall. Instinctively, she ran to him. "What is it Nissa. Is something wrong?" She asked desperately.

Nissa just shook his head. He didn't utter a word. At least he could manage that slight movement. His mother's appearance had a sudden mystical effect that called back life into his grossly mistreated body if only for a moment.

Sinee wasn't convinced. Something just didn't seem right. There was this eerie feeling running through her. It made her tense but she was paralyzed momentarily like many times before. A lot was familiar about this scene but something was a little unusual. If only she knew what.

Her handbag still hanging on her shoulder, she picked the boy up and carried him to the couch, her legs trembling with fright from something she didn't even know. His head rested on her lap as she ran her fingers through his dishevelled hair. She asked once more. "What's wrong sweetheart?"

Once more he shook his head.

Sinee didn't really need anyone to tell her what was wrong. Unless she had a selective memory, she could easily put two and two together. Something had greatly interfered with her cognitive capacity because she just wasn't doing the right thing.

Akkharat picked up a newspaper and slammed himself on the opposite seat. He was relaxed now. His heartbeat was back to normal. His eyes were on the same page for ages but his mind, really not. There was a lot of disgruntlement in his look, his breathing, his posture and just about everything. His wife could see it all.

"Where is Hansa?" She enquired politely of their second child. "Sleeping," answered a disinterested Akkharat.

"And the house-help?" "In the kitchen, I think."

With unspeakable feelings building up in her heart, she picked up her son and took him to bed.

A few moments later, she was in the living room. She sat next to Akkharat and holding up his head, she swivelled on the chair to place her laps under his head. Gently, she let it down to lie on her laps. That's what he wanted anyway. She was just living the life she had chosen. Sinee closed her eyes and tried to shield the dark fears clouding her mind.

Nissa was safely in bed. The poor boy didn't even look a bit like her son. Poor was the perfect word to describe him but the rest of the family didn't look so.

Before Akkharat's head was accustomed to the warmth on his wife's laps, the house-help came to the living room looking like one very desperate soul. Sinee didn't wait to be told what was wrong. "What is it Tida?" She asked as she shoved her husband off her laps. His newspaper went down to the floor. He almost went there with it.

"It's Nissa. I think he's very sick."

Frantically, Sinee and Tida rushed to his side. He had turned blue. "What is it Nissa?" His mother asked, tears flowing freely.

The boy didn't utter a word.

Proper instinct finally rushed back to her mind but way behind schedule. She quickly took him in her arms and rushed out. In the living room, Akkharat was still lying down reading his paper.

He had replaced her laps with a pillow. Not in the least did he seem perturbed. Just one look at him and Sinee knew that it was pointless seeking his help. She decided to take care of her burden. After all, only she knew where she got it from. "Get me my handbag Tida," she ordered.

The girl's response was swift. With her help, they put the boy in the front seat of his mother's car and buckled him up. "Take care of Hansa, will you?" Sinee asked though it pretty much sounded like an order. Whatever way her employer had intended it to be, she didn't mind.

Tida didn't acknowledge. She just stood there motionless and watched as the vehicle sped off. There was no doubt in Sinee's mind that Tida would do her will. But she just stood out there in the dark. She vowed to stay there until they were back. Nothing would move her, not even Hansa's cries. She had no reason to worry about Hansa but she was scared for the boy.

Somewhere near the hospital the boy finally spoke. "Mom!" He called.

Quickly, she took her eyes off the road. "Yes dear," she answered excitedly so hopeful that he was getting better.

Then came the shocker. He spoke slowly but calmly. "Dad kicked me in the tummy and banged my head against the wall," he explained briefly but precisely.

Sinee stretched out her hand to his cheeks and caressed him. "I'm so sorry son. This will never happen again. I'm going to leave him today." She promised her son and herself as well. She had promised herself that many times before but she had never promised her son that before. May be this time she would live up to her words.

"The boy has serious internal bleeding. We have to take him in for surgery right away." The doctor on call announced.

"Is there anything I can do?" Sinee wondered aloud. "Sure. Pray and pray a lot."

She embarked on it right away but her prayers were a little late. The boy died as they wheeled him to the theatre. His mother was right by his side. He tried saying bye to her but he was too feeble to. Sinee saw it coming and actually read his goodbye from his facial expressions.

"Don't! Please don't. Baby don't leave me," she cried out loud as she clutched his hand tighter while struggling to keep pace with the fast rolling stretcher.

Nissa shut his eyes for the last time and in his stead, his mother ended up in the ward.

5 DELAWARE, USA.

9.00 p.m.

All that Vin's family could ever want was at their disposal. They were proud to have Gibson as their surname. He had done everything to give them a good life. They had a good home in a safe neighbourhood and lots of love too. That was all so enviable but it didn't just rain down on them. There were lots of sacrifices but that was all history now. In fact, the tough times had all been washed out of their memories. Times had changed, washing ashore lots of welcome good fortunes. They now knew exactly what it meant to sleep on a bed of roses. They revelled in it and took great care to ensure they never had a reason to shed a single tear. Living life like they now did was a treasure they would do anything to protect.

That evening, Vin's family was all over the four bed roomed house but he was in the living room with his gorgeous wife Julia. They sat comfortably in each other's arms as they watched news on their favourite TV channel. No ill wind had ever been strong enough to wither their love and they too worked hard to ensure it never did. As they demonstrated their love to each other while keeping themselves updated with current affairs, they had no idea that the real news was just about to unfold in their own house.

Vin loved political news and followed them with a dedication that often amused his wife. She knew too well that politics captivated him and so she tried hard to create interest too. For her to be able to effectively support her dear husband, she had to be knowledgeable enough on the matter. She also knew about his aspirations for a seat in congress and was ready to play a lead role in his journey there.

The family didn't have a security guard. They didn't see the need. They lived in a very safe neighbourhood. That didn't mean that it was the least of their worries. They did have an electric fence and a burglar alarm linked to the police station, which was usually switched on when the family retired to bed. That was a huge mistake they were soon to learn about.

"Wsup old man." A loud deep and unpleasant voice came from behind them. He was startled and tried to turn round to see the person speaking to him but couldn't. A gun pressed hard against his neck. His wife loyally seated next to him managed to turn and couldn't hold back a shrieking scream.

"You do that again and you're dead." Another man warned.

Inside what they always considered to be a bastion of safety were four men all armed with guns. They looked ruthless and didn't need to repeat their warning. Two were left behind as the other two went round each room rounding up his three boys, daughter and the maid in the sitting room.

The whole family was terrified but Vin had to be brave. He pleaded with them to spare their lives. "Just tell me what you want and you'll have it."

The shorter man of them all appeared to hold authority. He was the one who dispensed orders. No one else spoke. Strangely, he spoke very fluent English. He sounded very educated. It was a big wonder why on earth he was doing this.

"You are a smart man Mr. Gibson. I admire old wise men."

"Thank you," Vin tried to grow the conversation. Maybe it would lead to some trust, understanding and hopefully, mercy. "I swear I will give you anything you want. Just don't harm us."

"Alright!" he went back sounding very compromising. "Let me start by introducing myself. You see, I already know you pretty well."

"Sure. Please go ahead."

"I'm best known as Terror. I have a degree in anthropology but who the hell wants to employ an anthropologist? Not you, not anyone. But my girlfriend has a degree in economics and you employed her. You gave her a lot of money and I suddenly lost meaning to her. She dumped me. So now I've come for some money too and a little extras."

"Alright, you can have all the money in the house and anything else you wish. If you'll allow me to get it for you," Vin said desperately.

"In due time. We are not in a hurry." Terror said as he walked closer to Vin's daughter. "What's your name beautiful?"

She looked at her father who in turn gave her an approving look then answered rather calmly, "Miriam."

"Mm! The name sounds beautiful too." Then he turned his attention to Vin. "Mr. Gibson, you offered me anything in this house and because of you, I don't have a girlfriend. So I've decided I want your daughter."

"No please. Not her," Julia pleaded for her only daughter.

"Shut up bitch! I'm not talking to you." Terror said furiously. He didn't like his decisions being questioned. His colleagues already knew that too well but Julia didn't. His mind was made up. It was the girl he wanted above all else.

"Listen," Vin started to negotiate. "I have a brand new Mercedes out there. You can have it instead."

"I was going to have the car anyway but your daughter will make a better prize." Terror said sarcastically then signalled to his colleagues who moved everyone else except Miriam closely together. They stood round pointing their guns at them. "One move or a sound and someone will be dead," he found himself at least kind enough to forewarn his captives.

Miriam trembled with fear. "Please.... please. " She was so struck with fright that she couldn't even finish her plea.

Terror held her by her neck and shoved her down to the floor. She started screaming but he fast plugged her mouth with a cloth. Without a care, he tore off her clothes and took a moment to laugh to himself. The frightened girl cuddled herself in a bid to hide her nudity. "Nice thing you sired here Mr. Gibson"

Julia closed her eyes in pain while the rest turned their eyes away as the short mad man went down on Miriam before the helpless family. They were too scared to utter a word but their hearts and minds were screaming for help. They witnessed in utter disbelief as Miriam was grossly violated. They could only share her pain with tears.

When he was done, he stood up and shamelessly applauded himself. "Wasn't I good beautiful?"

Miriam lay there in the same position he had left her. Only tears streaming from her fifteen year old eyes said something.

"Hey Snow," Terror called out to one of his men. "You can have the old bitch," he ordered. He actually prided himself to be very generous, which was why he decided to share out his spoils.

The man by the name Snow, quickly took the opportunity but Julia furiously fought back. Eventually he overwhelmed her and managed to tear off her clothes. She suffered the same fate as her daughter.

Vin could not take it anymore he had seen too much for a day. He was ready to give up his life for the sake of his family. The urgent will gave him courage to surprise the gangsters by snatching a gun from one. Without a second thought, he aimed it at the man proudly calling himself Terror. That was the man who had just raped his daughter-the daughter who was still laying helplessly on the floor. "Bang!" The shot went and the bullet shot through the man's heart.

Snow, the man who was still on top of his wife halted and ran for his dear life but a bullet was fast behind him. It quickly caught up with him on his back felling him down like a piece of old rotten useless log.

The others had little choice left. They could either stay and avenge their friends or make an escape. The escape was a wiser choice but they were daring enough to fire twice at their enemy. Vin too went down.

The paramedics later found three people on the floor. One had a crowd of scared souls around him. He was still breathing and after a quick examination and first aid, they declared, "he'll make it."

The other two people were carried out on stretchers but the smaller one was definitely lifeless. Probably, he was already where seven earnest prayers, especially Miriam's wished him to be-hell.

HERE AND AFTER

6
NOTHING BUT THE TRUTH

The spirit broke away from his body. There was a large tunnel of light– beaming white, leading up to a place he couldn't see yet. The light enveloped him and the path ahead but he couldn't see his way clearly. He took one look down at his lifeless body and decided he had no more need for it. Doctors were busy trying to bring his body back to life but he had already made up his mind. He didn't look back down again. He focused on what lay ahead and for some reason, he felt so free-it was unbelievable.

All the fears he had had before were all gone. He experienced a tranquility he had never known before. That was one thing he wouldn't mind more of. He looked up with unbridled anticipation as he went through the light.

Before he knew it, he had come to the end of the tunnel and before him was a river flowing east. His journey to the unknown suddenly came to a halt. All through his life on earth he had never learned to swim and there was no sign of a bridge. The river was very wide and its waters were flowing fast. It reminded him of the fear he had always had for water. He had two choices staring at him. Either turn back or attempt crossing the river. He reminded himself that he had vowed not to look back.

There were people on the banks of the river across. He looked closely and there was something very familiar about them. They were all his dead relatives, he realized. His father and mother were there, his four brothers, a sister, his uncles and aunts too. They were all beckoning him to cross the river chanting, "Be brave Edvaldo, be brave."

His father added, "We did it, you can do it too."

Edvaldo looked at the waters again. He certainly wasn't sure of it but his mother reassured him like she had always done, "you can make it son." Edvaldo wanted to ask her why she had to leave just when he needed her the most but he decided that the time wasn't appropriate.

"The water is shallow, just walk across." Someone

else added. Edvaldo was too busy sizing up the river to see who had said that, but it was his elder brother Niguel.

Finally, he put his best foot forward and quickly realized that the water wasn't as deep as he had imagined. The other foot found courage to follow and soon he was across. Motivated by the expectation of an ecstatic welcome on the other side, he concentrated on getting there-his eyes staying true and faithful to the water. They couldn't trust the water enough to stray up even for a second.

All his efforts concentrated on getting to the other side the soonest possible but something no experience had prepared him for eagerly awaited to shatter his confidence. There was no jamboree to welcome him as anticipated. All those relatives who had given him the courage to cross where his usually strong will wouldn't let him, were nowhere in sight to welcome him. They had all vanished into thin air but the way ahead was much clearer than before. A crystal ball wouldn't give him a clearer picture of the ground that awaited his feet. Something told him that they hadn't abandoned him but had only allowed him to make the rest of the journey alone. He took a look back and saw his lifeless body being covered up by a doctor who declared without the slightest trace of emotion, "He's dead. Take him away." Right then he knew that he had to be brave enough to make it the rest of the way-a way he had no idea where it led. Something seemed to whisper to him that he had nothing to fear. Whatever it was, it gave him a desperately needed reassurance that something wonderful lay in waiting.

The river he had just crossed was now raging, its

waters flowing rapidly and fiercely. He knew he couldn't go back. Fear of facing the distance he had already covered rather than what lay ahead made his legs weak.

He came to a massive and stunningly beautiful gate. This gate was different from all others he had ever seen. It wasn't made of wrought iron but of pure gold wonderfully crafted into the most magnificent thing he had ever laid his curious eyes on. He could see through the gate. A road led away from it, passing through a garden filled with succulent ripe fruits. It too was constructed with gold tiles that were laid in an intricate and amazingly spellbinding pattern. Such a road could only be walked on by a fastidiously chosen few. One had to be extremely blessed for his feet to step on it.

Beyond the gate, he could see large equally remarkable houses way ahead. People mingled with angels and they all marched and sang happily. These people seemed free of any pain, worries or misery. There was incredible happiness written all over their faces. Rather peculiar were their looks. They all looked young and vibrant with health, energy and enthusiasm. Though he was on the other side of the gate, he could feel the vibrant atmosphere that gave him the feeling that he was amongst them. The mood was too good and infectious to resist. This was the place Edvaldo wanted to be. If he couldn't be with the family he loved, then he'd rather be here.

An angel stood guard at the gate. He had never seen one before but he just knew he was one. Besides, he matched the imaginations he had always had of them perfectly well. The angel saw the curiosity and anticipation in his face or maybe he read it in his mind. He was an angel after all. "This is heaven where there's no suffering but eternal life and happiness." Slowly but surely he informed Edvaldo. "Before I check if you appear in the books, please look back at how you spent the life God kindly blessed you with."

Edvaldo turned and looked back but he didn't see anything. "Please have a seat. This might take a while." The angel politely asked him.

A seat Edvaldo hadn't noticed before was there before him. He went round and nervously sat down as he anxiously awaited the next instructions. He was eager to know what the heavens thought of the way he had lived his life. Nothing appeared to disturb him. He certainly didn't live like an angel. God didn't make him one anyway but he was satisfied that he had done his best on earth.

"Look up in the sky Edvaldo."

A bit puzzled, he looked up and there in the sky his life on earth flashed before him. It was like a cinema with a giant screen and an audience of only one. The fifty-nine years he had spent on the most popular planet started rolling.

Nothing was exceptional about his childhood. Of course he had lots of love. Being the last-born, that wasn't out of expectation. Love came his way from all directions right from his parents and siblings to people he had to keep on being reminded exactly how they were related. All that love was never taken for granted. He returned it back with a generous share of his own.

While others couldn't go to school because of lack of fees, he had no excuse not to get the education he craved for. God had reserved many blessings for him including a substantial share of the grey matter. Like every other young man, he longed for schooling to end so he could really start living. The other side of the world looked sweeter and very attractive. Still, he had to acquire enough education to guarantee its sweetness wouldn't turn bitter at some point. When all the schooling was done, he found a job that could pay for the kind of living he wanted. For a while he wasn't happy that he didn't get the career of his dreams. He just didn't want to understand that there were good reasons for it, until many years later. Like many other young men, he was impatient with God. He couldn't understand why God didn't answer his prayers and reward his efforts. Maybe he didn't answer those prayers the way he expected them to be but he sure did reward his efforts, if only he could just open up his eyes and see it. Besides, there was a plan to be followed and it wasn't Edvaldo's.

High schools were very few in a country that had just kicked out the Portuguese masters but he made it to one. For six years he had attended a prestigious but strict catholic high school. No one could spare his or her fancy for him not only because of his likeable nature but also because he was bright and obedient. Everyone lay their trust on him. The school added a hand to his gentlemanly character. He was always ready to help but aided by his natural humbleness, he was trimmed to be more than a gentleman.

Edvaldo certainly could never be described as an extrovert but he wasn't an introvert either. He was amazingly friendly to just about everyone. He didn't strictly speak much but he was always very jovial. And when things weren't good, he just kept quiet. That maybe was a weakness that often ate at his heart. When aggravated, he just kept quiet and not many

would ever know. But he was a patient man –
sometimes a little too much. One characteristic that
no one would ever forget about him was his humility.
He was probably the most humble living being.

Luck continued hovering over him wherever he
went. As he kept changing calendars, his fortunes
kept on piling. He had been blessed with lots of
wealth, which he gladly shared with everyone in need.
But towards his last years, his angel of fortune
decided to move on to a new client. His heart still
remained as big as ever. Against all expectations, he
remained the same humble and friendly gentleman he
had always been.

A couple of days into his fifty-eighth year since
pushing through into this unforgiving world, he drove
to town as carefully as ever. He was on his way to
attend to some urgent work oblivious of the fact that
he was also on another journey that he least expected.
His clock had only a little longer than a year before it
stopped ticking but he didn't know it, yet.

There was no indication that parts in his healthy
looking body were getting dangerously worn out. If
life only had lights and signs along the way to prepare
one for situations ahead he'd be well armed for the
journey ahead. There was that one time that he
blacked out at one of his homes. That was one very
isolated case and there was someone out there to
immediately lay the blame on, some mosquito-
transmitted parasite. The real killer got away scot-free
giving it ample time to wreak havoc on its
unsuspecting victim.

This time, its harm well done, it was bold enough
to come out clear. But he had never been to med
school. What someone with a title other than Mr. or

Ms. could've easily identified escaped this very knowledgeable mind. All he could see was a blurred vision that split the vehicles ahead into three parts of each.

He joked about it later that evening. "My eyes are getting better," he said in his usual jovial style. Instead of one, I've been seeing three vehicles ahead."

"You're not serious," his daughter Flavia said with her characteristic concern.

Edvaldo was funny too and at the end of it all, all his family laughed it off not knowing they were laughing his lovely smile away.

Day three with the same problem and his son-in-law Silvanio was worried. He had known from experience not to take health matters lightly. His father, believing that he was too strong, belittled diseases. That attitude eventually landed him into a hell of trouble. That trouble was a stroke that left his entire right side unable to obey his commands. Silvanio feared the same for his father-in-law. "I really think you should see a doctor," he urged with deep concern.

"Sure. First thing tomorrow." His smile wasn't convincing but Silvanio read some concern behind it.

Edvaldo had already figured out what to blame his recent blurred vision on. It had to be his age. Going by the national life expectancy figure, he certainly wasn't young. Who didn't know that something happened to eyes as age caught up? His only worry was the two thousand or so Real he'd have to part with for a pair of spectacles. That amount could reduce his worries for one of his children's college fees. He couldn't afford to waste even a Centavo. Things were not as easy as they used to be. His pockets had grown too shallow for his responsibilities. He could only reminisce with a smile the long gone days when he could pay fees for scores of needy children. Gladly, he acknowledged that life had its own ups and downs. It's only unfortunate that his downs came too late in life.

Careful not to stir more concern, or find himself driving into a ditch, he kept his promise to see a doctor just so his children would stop worrying. But he chose the wrong doctor. "There's nothing wrong with your eyes, sir." The ophthalmologist declared only to receive a gaze from a very surprised Edvaldo. "There's something wrong though with your blood pressure," he added hoping it would wipe away that handsome gaze and summon some big concern.

He played with his head a little side to side, something he loved doing then asked with a broad smile, "What?"

The doctor wasn't looking to alarm him but he had to assign it the necessary urgency. "It's too high," he said rather coldly. "You should see Dr Lucio at Alexandre Bernicia hospital right away."

"Right away?"

"Yes, right away." The seriousness in his looks, words, tone and even posture were enough to send the patient running.

That was only a few hundred meters away. He had only been to the hospital once before to see a brother- in-law who unfortunately didn't make it out alive. The rest he saw of it was in the Television news. It could pass for the most filmed hospital in the country. That's where all the rich and mighty visited for medical attention.

He drove himself there against advice. Besides, he

didn't feel sick at all. Dr. Lucio couldn't believe the pressure readings. He called in an associate to confirm it.

"It's amazing that you're still walking. That pressure is not for a living person. You have to be hospitalized immediately."

"No, No." He was quick to refuse. "We can't let you go, I'm sorry."

"Okay. Let me go and look for money then come back," realizing that he won't win, he suggested.

"That's highly unadvisable. You can take care of that later when you are well."

That was one hospital for the wealthiest guys in the country and right now, he wasn't one of them. Another more affordable hospital would serve the need equally well. The doctors were too concerned for his life than they were for his pockets. They just wouldn't let him go. Okay, they really didn't think he would make it far with that kind of pressure. Though they couldn't say it, they really thought that he was a dead man walking.

"All right, let me call my boss first," he pleaded. He no longer worked for the secretariat of the federal revenue of Brazil. Things in the private sector were very different.

"Why don't you give us the number and we'll call him. You really need to be on a bed receiving medication."

Eventually, the doctors got him where they strongly felt he should've been. Edvaldo couldn't recall ever being on a hospital bed but he acknowledged that there had to be a first time. He didn't need reminding that he wasn't super human. So for decades he had challenged the fiddle at fitness, it didn't mean he'd be successful forever.

Droves of relatives and friends soon came calling. Their fears quickly quelled, a great thanks to his jokes that found a place even in the darkest of his moments. All worries flew out of the window a little too quickly. That was perfectly fine. What one didn't know certainly couldn't hurt. Why shed tears then when their purpose had months to come. A little joke here, a smile there and a trademark laugh saved the tears for later.

Lots of tests were done and everyone kept asking what the results were. Edvaldo had a polite and smart way of avoiding a topic but this time, that wasn't a fete he could manage for long. Not especially when he had to be taken to theatre for a minor operation. He just had to part with some explanations.

"Well...the doctors joined some veins on my hand." "Why?" Almost everyone wanted to know.

He chuckled a bit but the expressions on his children's faces weren't compromising. They wanted to know the truth about their father's health.

"They say I might need dialysis at some point in the future. The surgery was a preparation for that."

He had won. For now everybody believed he was all right. The future could be ten, twenty or even thirty years away. Was it?

Edvaldo had parted with some selective truth, not all the truth. For now, everyone was back laughing to his stories and jokes. That was more important to him than ever before.

The story he didn't tell was that his kidneys were badly damaged. But he heartily told the one about how fit his heart was, the liver and all the other vital organs. He conveniently forgot to say that he might soon need a transplant to replace the damaged pair. Both were failing and unfortunately, too fast for him to think straight about it.

Who would donate that kidney anyway? It most probably had to be one of his children. No, he wouldn't entertain such a thought. Not those children he had gone through so much pain for. The voice at the back of his mind persistently reminded him that he had lived his life to the fullest. He just wouldn't endanger his child's life to live for a minute longer. What if that one kidney he'd leave the child with one day failed? He'd never be comfortable even in heaven. So there would be problems with him gone. May be some would not finish college but one day, maybe they would understand his silence.

Later, he went home and formulated a will in his mind. He then took titles of his properties and kept them safely at the homes of those he wanted to gift them to when he was gone. All went back to normal. Everybody forgot that someone in the family was sick. Well, Edvaldo had been given a full explanation of what was going on inside his body. He was a grown man anyway. It was very difficult to accept something one only saw and heard on TV's medical dramas and thought it never happened for real. Yes those dreaded words from doctors about life that gave time limits had been put straight to his ears. His kidneys had a problem but not his ears. What he heard was true.

"Soon we'll be your neighbours. We need to move to some place near the airport so that I won't need to wake up early," Edvaldo told to his son-in-law.

"All the better so we won't have to miss you like we do," he applauded the decision. They were very good friends and could talk for hours about things they shared interest in, as well as the business they intended to start that August.

The frequency at which he repeated his wish to move was a little unusual. Silvanio wondered if there was more to those words.

As days went by, he became more specific. "I think we'll move there in August."

Then came an evening when Edvaldo wasn't feeling very well and Silvanio went to see him. They were more of friends than in-laws. But then, he was a friend to everyone.

When time came for Silvanio to leave, his father-in-law insisted on escorting him. A few uncomfortable moments before they bid each other goodbye, Silvanio was certain that there was something his father-in-law wanted to say to him only he never quite did. If only he knew how to make him comfortable enough to say it.

"I'll come for a cup of tea tomorrow evening and then we can discuss one or two issues." That's all he managed to say.

"Sure that'd really be nice."

That was a date Edvaldo couldn't forget. He spent the day looking forward to the evening and when it finally came, he went home got rid of the tie and changed to a more comfortable black leather jacket. It matched very well with the black pair of trousers and the brilliant white shirt.

As usual, no one could stop him from removing his shoes. He didn't want to add a single grain of dust to the same carpet his two grandsons played on. The second grandson was actually named after him, which made him very proud. At least he had seen four grandchildren-two girls and two boys. The girls had come first to two of his daughters, Isadora and Denisa. Then Flavia gave the two grandsons Alanzo and Luis. Edvaldo's first two names were actually Edvaldo Luis. Luis had been born just about the time when his life started draining out. Alanzo had been named after Edvaldo's long-time friend and now in-law who fondly called him Sir Edvaldo. Well, Edvaldo also called him Sir Alanzo. It was always fun watching them call each other Sir this and Sir that.

During the visit, Flavia took two photos of her father with his two grandsons oblivious that those would be historical photos.

Alanzo who was about three had a huge passion for soft drinks and whenever he saw his grandfather, he knew one would be coming. He'd run to him exclaiming, "Soda! Soda! Soda!" Granddad would always send for one.

It was no different this time. He called the maid and instructed, "Can you bring Alanzo a bottle of Sprite." He always insisted on Sprite. The rest he said were too sweet for the baby or had too much gas.

The girl took the money from his hand and ran to do his bidding.

Throughout that evening nothing extraordinary was said. After all the talks and laughs, Silvanio and his first son Alanzo escorted him to his car. Edvaldo placed Alanzo on his laps and allowed him to play with the steering wheel for a while. A little later he drove off leaving Silvanio wishing he had prompted Edvaldo to say what was on his mind.

A couple of weeks on, he arrived from a holiday

trip in the evening not in good shape and went to see his doctor.

After a few tests, they strongly recommended that he go to a better hospital for very specialized tests and treatment. With his condition, there wasn't much they could do. The following morning he woke up and dressed up formally hoping to pass by the hospital, get treatment and proceed to work as usual. It didn't go quite as planned because once again he was immediately hospitalized.

The whole family was there to see him during the visiting hours. He seemed quite okay and didn't arouse a shred of worry in his family. Vicente the first-born had always liked bullying his sister Flavia. This time, he grabbed her by the neck and directed her towards the balcony. Maybe their father noticed something with Silvanio or it's something he had always observed whenever something of the sort happened. This time he didn't keep quiet about it.

"Tell him she's yours now. He should be careful with the way he handles her," he told his son-in-law in a concerned but jovial way.

"It's high time he knew that," Silvanio agreed. It was an accurate observation and he couldn't go on forever denying that he didn't like it.

The day Edvaldo was finally discharged from hospital, he was very happy to go home. He walked around conversing with his visitors, most of whom were his family. His daughters Agnese and Elvita stood together with their brother-in-law Silvanio. He approached them and joked a little.

"So what do the doctors say?" Silvanio enquired.

"Aha! They say my kidneys are no good." Anyone could have thought he was saying something really nice.

Silvanio was actually more worried about the other single organs like the heart. "At least you can live with one kidney or get a transplant," he answered with some relief.

"Of course, Agnese can give me half a kidney and Elvita the other half," he trivialized the matter and they all laughed over something they shouldn't have.

Before he left, he went to thank the nurses and wish them well. "Thank you," he said in Brazilian Portuguese, which he relished speaking in, and apparently was very fluent in. "We are very grateful for everything," he said with his hands so humbly held together at the front.

That was characteristic of him. He was too liberal with the words 'thank you' and 'please'. It didn't matter the situation, the person or even their age. It didn't matter that it was his right. He still said 'thank you' in the most humble way.

Leaving the nurses amazed, he went to the vehicle in Flavia's arms and home to prepare for dialysis.

The following Saturday was the last day in that cold July. His daughter Flavia, her husband and first son Alanzo went to visit. Alanzo got his Sprite as usual but that was a very important bottle of Sprite. Nobody knew it yet but that green colour of the bottle probably meant it was time to go. Fine, go where and who. And why didn't all the other times Edvaldo had bought his grandson that drink mean anything? Why only this time? Only God knew. Grandfather too had at least an idea and since then, Alanzo never asked for soda again. With that 300ml of sparkling liquid, his obsession and taste for sodas suddenly died.

Edvaldo was very disappointed that the family had left Luis behind. He really wanted to see him but the weather and the distance had conspired against his wishes. Besides, Flavia was working that morning and her husband couldn't handle the two alone to town where they were to link up. Leaving the five-month-old baby behind was one thing the couple would later live to regret.

Vicente was away. He'd been sent to liquefy some assets so as to take care of his father's treatment. All the other children were around.

As usual, Edvaldo ensured chicken was served. His grandson was allergic to red meat and had to have the best at his grandfather's house.

"It's time you seriously reduced your travelling, at least skip some weekends and send Vicente instead," Silvanio suggested during a conversation.

"Oh yes. From now on I'll just be sitting here watching telly instead."

"You've promised that many times before but you have never honoured it."

"This time I promise I'm going to take a serious rest. You'll see."

"That'll be good and you can watch this programme called 'The Africans' by Professor Ali Mazrui. You'll enjoy it. It's on Sundays so tomorrow you can catch it." Silvanio said.

"Sure I will."

True he had all the intentions of watching it but he didn't. It sounded just like the kind of programme he loved to watch. Early Sunday morning, Flavia's mom called to say his health had deteriorated. He couldn't move an inch on his own. August had begun on a terrible note.

He had been quite weak on the Saturday having to struggle to stand up and making some very wobbly steps. But he wouldn't accept assistance. Silvanio thought it was a side effect of the numerous pills he was taking. Probably also the reason he was so irritable, something very uncharacteristic of him.

Silvanio dressed up and dashed out of the house. Until then, he didn't know he could be that fast. On the way, he made frantic calls to organize for transport. Fortunately Hernandez, another of Edvaldo's sons-in-law had a vehicle and was already on his way there.

Edvaldo had already issued a crisp order for his brother and nephew to be summoned and everybody wondered why. Words had no trouble flowing out but he couldn't move a single muscle.

Lying on his bed, he said to Silvanio, "I feel so weak."

That didn't need saying. He certainly looked so. Silvanio had trouble making meaning out of life if such a nice man could be so helpless. There was no time to make sense out of anything. He joined hands with Hernandez and Cidro, Edvaldo's son to get him into the vehicle. Hernandez's brother joined them along the way in another vehicle. They needed all the assistance they could get. At the hospital as they got him out of the green Hyundai, he audibly preferred death to troubling people that much.

"No, don't say that," Hernandez urged him.

It took many painstaking hours to get him out of casualty to the ward. They couldn't even get him to the private ward where he had been two days before. The ridiculous reason those underpaid government hospital staff could offer was that the cash office at the private ward wasn't open on Sundays and no one could be admitted without paying a deposit. All that nonsense and yet the hospital owed him money? They couldn't even trace his file. So the solution they could offer was to take him to the public wards till Monday when they could transfer him to the private ward. Silvanio couldn't help wishing he had ready cash to pay a deposit for him at a private hospital where attention would be immediate. He knew then that it was a terrible thing to be poor or well, broke.

Edvaldo preferred his head held up a little high but the damn bed he lay on didn't have support for the headrest. So Hernandez, his brother, Silvanio and Cidro took turns to support it.

It was already evening when they finally got him to a ward. As soon as they had wheeled him into the ward, the guards wanted them out. Visiting hours were over and the guards wouldn't hear their requests for a little time with him.

"No way!" They protested.

The two guards, ill equipped with public relations skills found themselves in the unenviable position of being confronted by a gang of angry relatives who had been through a long agonizing day. They proved to be chicken-hearted and had no choice but to turn a blind eye to the rules they loved enforcing. Eventually, Flavia's mom gave Edvaldo some few bites of the supper that was served way before the sun kissed the horizon. The food had little appeal to the eye. It had no aroma and it probably tasted horrible. It's no wonder that Edvaldo preferred the bottled water that Silvanio helped him sip.

"You better get well. I want you to be strong enough to beat me in arm wrestling tomorrow,"

Silvanio said to him.

"Definitely." He responded with a smile that was hard to tell what it really meant.

Soon it was time to leave. Visiting hours were long over but Edvaldo's brother and nephew whom he had summoned stayed behind. They took so long that Hernandez, Silvanio and Cidro went back to see what was keeping them.

Miraculously, Edvaldo had suddenly gained so much strength that he was walking himself to the gents. As he walked back, he noticed the three young men. He stopped for a moment in time to catch their speechless expressions. Looking a little confused he said to them, "Sorry for the trouble." But he really needn't apologize for they didn't feel he had troubled them in any way. They could do more if they could and they made sure they let him know that.

"Sorry for the trouble." Those were words that would keep resounding in their minds forever. Those apologetic sentiments were the words they would last remember him with.

The picture soon vanished from the sky leaving it as blue as before. Edvaldo turned to the angel standing closely beside him with his hand resting reassuringly over his shoulders. Past the angel, there was something excitingly different. The golden gates stood wide open. That must have been a good sign and Edvaldo didn't know if to jump up and down in jubilation or to cry. Some big portion of him still wanted to be back with his family. With slow gesticulations, the angel ushered him in. Another man with a brighter glow than the angel's and who appeared to be too superior stood at the gate's threshold. He held out his hand to Edvaldo and said,

"I am the way, the truth and the life: no man cometh unto the father, but by me."

Edvaldo quickly remembered those words from the book of John 14:6 and knew that that was Jesus holding out his hand to him. Without hesitation, he accepted it.

"Welcome to heaven Edvaldo," the angel said. "The good you did on earth has opened the gates wide for you."

Two weeks later on the fourteenth day of that sad August, his body was laid to rest but his soul already had eternal peace. If only he was there to see the crowd at his funeral. "Was he a politician," someone wondered.

"No. He was just a very nice man," another answered his curiosity.

e.

7 SOMETHING LIKE THE TRUTH

KERUBO

A little after she had laboured for the third child, her world started to crumble. There was no one to glue it back together to its original state. Someone had turned off the lights from her world and she couldn't see where she was going anymore.

She was almost about to start counting years for her little baby. The months were ticking by fast and so was her life. Kerubo wasn't what many people would call much. She was just a housewife. The name was a little demeaning to her. It sounded like she was of no good to the society. Bringing up three children all within five years range was more work than most people could handle. With no remuneration at the end of a hard day's work, the economists didn't like considering that kind of work in their gross domestic product calculations. Adding up children to the already congested world only presented them with more problems. But she also did something that would please the economists from the precincts of her house.

Between that and the kids, she hardly ever found time for herself. When she did, usually on weekends, she liked to pamper herself with a long relaxing bath. She could dip her body in some warm water and remain there for over an hour. If only she knew that that occasional little indulgence kept beckoning the greatest nightmare of her life.

She could take her hat off for her husband Tim anytime. He was very loving and caring and the best father she could have for her children. He always found time to help with the babies so she could have some time to herself and would take as much time as possible apart from this one time.

Kerubo wanted to give some of that time to Tim. She wanted to surprise him but the surprise was already reserved for her.

Something seemed a little strange as she left the bathroom wrapped in a towel. She couldn't hear a sound from any of her children making her believe that they must've been asleep. There was soft music playing in her bedroom but as she approached it she could pick some unusual noises. Noises she thought only she made, at least in that house. She couldn't be more wrong. She'd forgotten that she didn't have monopoly to the sensations that squeezed out those noises.

Her feet suddenly grew cautious as they advanced nearer to her room. The door was ajar. She didn't even need to step in to see the horror she wished she never did and wasn't meant to see anyway.

Her house help Nancy was the source of those noises. The girl lay shamelessly sprawled up all naked on her precious bed. Even more disgusting was the act she was so happily engaged in. Tim was the cause of her screams and they weren't screams of pain.

It was obvious nothing was being forced into her. She had wanted it and was participating fully in harvesting a fruit from a tree she didn't own. The kind of passion they had told Kerubo that this wasn't the first time they were having each other. It was a two-way joy, wasn't it?

Kerubo just couldn't believe that it was Tim giving her house help the one thing he had vowed six years before never to give to anyone else but her. She didn't know what to do. Her legs wouldn't move her closer and her eyes were terrified of getting a closer look. She was dumbfounded but her heart was screaming. How could this happen? What had she done to deserve it?

Those were questions she couldn't find answers for. Shock did strange things to her. She wanted to scream but she couldn't. Finally, her feet took her back to the bathroom. She pulled off the towel and looked through the mirror. Did she look so bad? She wondered. Did the kid's mess up her looks so bad that the only male angel she knew would be tempted to stray?

Kerubo stayed in the bathroom the period she should've stayed in the first place all the time trying to answer questions she simply couldn't.

She should've known better. She even managed to lay some of the blame on herself. That girl always seemed to dress a little too inappropriately but she did nothing about it. Why anyway? She never saw Tim's eyes notice it. He had eyes only for her. So she always thought.

A long while later there was a knock at the door. "Hey, what's happening?" Tim asked. "You've stayed there too long today. Is everything alright?" He was concerned as ever.

"Sorry. Got a little carried away," she answered quite calmly while trying to fight back loads of tears crowding up her eyes.

Tim loyally stood there talking to her until she flung the door open. He looked really handsome and smart. "You look stunning," he expressed his admiration like he did every other day.

"Thanks," she went back while wondering why he had to sleep with someone else if she was really that stunning. Never in a million years would she have guessed that her angel of a husband was sleeping around. She didn't know him anymore. Who knows how many others he was finding time to get into.

"I have to meet some friends. I'll be back soon." Tim announced as he kissed his wife goodbye.

Nancy sat in the sitting room staring at them as if

telling Kerubo that she had already had him and now he didn't need her company.

Tim left without any suspicion but when he went back three hours later, his accomplice wasn't there. "Where's Nancy?" He wondered after staying a while without seeing her.

"I don't know," Kerubo retorted. A little while later, he repeated the same question. It was getting late in the night and he couldn't help thinking something wasn't right. Who wouldn't be concerned about someone who supplied him with so much good stuff? "Why don't you go and look for her in the streets where she belongs?" Kerubo answered repulsively. She almost lost her temper.

That statement didn't say much but it didn't say little either. Tim just had to piece together the puzzle by himself.

The following Monday, Tim took up the skin of another animal. He came home from work that evening and made an announcement Kerubo would never forget. It was more devastating than what she had witnessed. "I've decided to take another wife and I'm spending the night with her today," he said shamelessly.

That was too much bad news for one sentence but she remained composed. "Let me guess," she surprised him. "It's Nancy and you have already rented a house for her."

Tim didn't answer back but his silence was enough confirmation. Kerubo was wondering how an angel could turn wild so abruptly.

Having a co-wife was one thing, but one that had once been her house help was another. She never asked to be helped on wifely duties. But it was done.

Tim got Nancy a job at his place of work. They now slept together and worked together. He had made few mistakes in his life but marrying Nancy was his greatest of all. It made up for all the other mistakes he should've made before.

Nancy was quite pretty and she made him happy. She had to make him happy anyway. It was part of the grand plan that pitted her mother and her against unsuspecting Tim. To them, a man was a thing to have, a husband the better but a rich one was worth shedding off the wolf's skin at any cost. Tim was fairly well off and both Nancy and her cunning mother wanted a fair share of that wealth. That's all they saw when they looked at him.

Almost fifteen years down the line, a series of misfortunes wiped out the wealth. He couldn't take care of her expensive taste anymore and that didn't win him much friendship with her body. Not even the title husband, which she had since formalized, could give him the right to it. She only gave it to those who could afford to pamper her with hard currency.

Dan could do all that. He was her boss and a good friend of her husband. What she denied Tim, she gave out liberally to Dan who didn't care that she was his friend's wife as long as she didn't care either. Besides, he paid very dearly for that stolen pleasure with his immense wealth.

At least there was kerubo to turn to. She wouldn't deny him anything if he wanted it even if she was on her dying bed. She took him in her arms and anywhere else he wanted. Breaking her vows wasn't something she was about to start doing. She still belonged to him even though she'd spent fifteen years sharing him with someone she despised.

Rumours started spreading and soon everyone at work knew about the illicit relationship Nancy and Dan were engaged in. Tim could only pretend he knew nothing of the loud whispers.

Dan's mind started getting adventurous. He really didn't care if his friend knew what he was doing behind his back. Even worse, he started feeling that if he could have one of his wives then he could have them all. He had the money, the power and the looks too. Tim's money and power were all gone and Dan believed women didn't think looks made a man. He didn't see anything to stop him from having Kerubo too.

When Dan went visiting alone during office hours, Kerubo welcomed him well. She even made a cup of tea for him, which he hurriedly took. He moved closer and laid a hand on her lap then hell broke loose. She slapped him so hard that he almost shed some tears. His crafty mind lied to him that threats would make her budge.

"You know I can have your husband fired if you don't give me what I want," he tried out some intimidation.

"And what is it that you want?" She retorted without a care.

"Don't be silly. Want me to spell it out?" Wearing a smile that Kerubo thought to be very ugly, he answered.

Kerubo nodded with rage. "Yes. You can try spelling it then get the hell out of my house. Isn't it enough the hurt you have caused your friend with Nancy?"

"Enough!" He too got furious. "Have you any idea who is keeping the auctioneers away? This house could have been long gone if it wasn't for me."

"We can survive without a house. We didn't even have one when we came to the city anyway. Now get out," she ordered with an uncompromising tone.

The tone told Dan that he was shooting his ball in the wrong direction. He stood up and started towards the door saying, "You'll regret this."

"I can never regret not answering to your whims. I'd rather die first."

"Oh! You will. But I'm a good man. I'll give you twenty four hours to reconsider," he said as he chuckled to himself and looking rather silly.

Twenty four hours came and went. His threat came through. Tim was sacked for something he didn't do and the house was sold to recover money loaned to Dan that it had secured. He just plainly refused to pay the debt while he could even clear it with a single cheque. Tim tried turning to Nancy for help but she gave him the best of her back. She refused to let Tim stay in her house swearing she could never support a man. She would not even serve him with food when he went by to see his children.

The only option left for Tim and his first wife was to go back to their motherland, something that for some very weird reason seemed to amuse Nancy so much. Life turned into a nightmare but Kerubo struggled at the farm to give it hope and hope was always close by.

After watching her entire life pass by through her eyes, the angel said to her, "the gates of heaven won't open for you yet. Your purpose on earth is not yet done. Go back and finish it."

Life slowly squeezed back into her lifeless body. The tears and the screams from family and neighbours suddenly died off.

8 NOTHING LIKE THE TRUTH

ALISA

The first epistle of John tells us not to love the
world, or the things that are in the world. It warns
that if any man loves the world, the love of the father
is not in him for all that is in the world, the lust of the
flesh, and the lust of the eyes, and the pride of life, is
not of the Father, but of the world. The entire world

shall pass away, and the lust as well but he that does the will of God has forever.

Way before she finished primary school she was already very aware of the bewitching effect she had on boys. No one could argue about it. She was damn beautiful. There wasn't even a tiny scar on her skin. She was simply flawless with a complexion that almost matched the evening sun in colour. Kid gloves were used on her from the moment she arrived on earth and she learned to use the same on herself. It was no wonder that the only scars she had had something to do with ensuring that she stayed alive. They were so few that she could point them all out in seconds. All were associated with vaccinations. That was okay, she didn't mind it at all because she just couldn't imagine the dazzling package she was, being immobilized by something like polio. Boys adored her and even her male teachers gave her some attention that she knew too well had nothing to do with her interests but theirs.

Then came high school and along came Marek. He was a little older and through with high school. At first glance, Alisa didn't think much of him but he was kind of a village celebrity. Every other girl seemed to have already been made a jewel in his crown. She was about the only one left to join the queue to his bed. That wasn't necessarily good because almost no one had the guts to ask her out let alone ask to have what she had. Not that she really wanted to give it to him but she wanted to know what was so special about the guy.

Anticipation was getting the better of her while he was just exercising patience as part of his plan. While she agonized about why he hadn't made a move on her like everyone else, he had already made her his pet project just waiting to be executed. He didn't need a feasibility study on her or any other girl. He only needed a one on one opportunity and her curiosity would be washed off.

Competition was however too close, as close as the next bed in her room. That was fine because she was ready to counter any competition with everything she had. If she placed everything she had on the table, she didn't think anybody else had a prayer.

From the moment he said the first words to her she was hooked. She started singing his tune and sung it really well. Alisa was beautiful but others were too in their own unique ways. Before she could pronounce the word love, she was deeply in it. But

Marek's interest span was very short and he wasn't the kind to be tied down. He had a reputation to uphold even though to most guys it sounded too glossy to be true while to the girls it sparked off huge fires inside them.

Trapping him in her world didn't come for a song as anticipated. It wasn't easy but she eventually won his heart then later his body fell prey too. Stealing away is heart was one thing but keeping his body prey was a whole different dance. She had to give out lots of hers and at times in ways that not even the sleazy magazines could teach her. Even before he had the urge to have himself a girl she was already giving herself lest he quenched that urge on some other girl. Like she had once promised herself, she wrapped him up around her little finger. If Eve could get her way around Adam, so could Alisa on Marek. Soon Marek was a totally different man-a one-woman man.

A couple of years later she rediscovered her

former glory. Guys at work reawakened it and suddenly she wanted Marek out of her life. He had outlived his purpose and now had become a menace especially to her freedom, which incidentally she was the one who had meticulously defined for both of them. It served her quite well then but now that there was all this attention, attraction and seduction, her curiosity was awakened. Suddenly she found life with one man boring.

Marek reluctantly stepped aside but only for a while. He had no doubts about his prowess. Though a little rusty after years out of practice, his tongue could still get girls racing to answer to his whims. Alisa soon realized that and came calling back. She was jealous and confused. She didn't want Marek anymore and yet she didn't want anyone else to have him. This time she had to lay a permanent claim on the guy and soon he was answering yes to the priest's question.

Marriage could not take them back to where they were before things became sour. There was a need that she had foregone and it came back to haunt their marriage later. Marek had to beg for things that both God and the law recognized as his basic right from their union. It was really a pity for him. A benefit that went with marriage wasn't in this package. All he got was a very beautiful woman that made him the envy of all men. But he'd rather not be praised for the prize and be happy. His prize was like a nicely wrapped gift box with nothing inside.

Alisa was jealously protective and wouldn't give him the space to seek temporary reprieves elsewhere. She didn't give him what he wanted and didn't want anyone to give it to him either.

That really puzzled Marek. He had signed up for a

life of happiness. Yes he was warned that there would be ups and downs but no one told him the downs would start so soon or last forever. He had vows to keep which made him wonder when else he was supposed to be happy. It certainly didn't seem like it'd ever be on this earth, probably after he was dead.

A day came when Alisa's age read thirty-five and something happened to her. She got her drive back in arrears. Marek couldn't be there every day to take care of it. He was working a hundred and ten kilometers away and could only be there on weekends.

Unlike her husband, Alisa wasn't ready to put her happiness on hold for a single day. When Marek wasn't there to take care of her physical needs, she'd pick the one she fancied from the many who were dying to do it. Ondrej, her boss and Pastor Domino were just some of them, but the Pastor particularly gave her a thrill she could never explain. And when the two stood before heaven's gates, they wouldn't open.

The angel reminded them what Romans 6:23 said, a verse that the Pastor as well as the regular churchgoer Alisa knew too well. He spoke pitifully, "for the wages of sin is death; but the gift of God is eternal life through Jesus Christ our lord."

The grounds below their feet opened up and they sunk into an eternal furnace.

9 SOMETHING VERY TRUE

NISSA

Sinee. Everyone knew the name of the new girl in school. The reason wasn't entirely because she was new but also because she was stunning. Even the biggest skeptics wouldn't deny that she was overly blessed with the looks but not many people knew of the extra beauty in her voice. Her words were very rare but very softly and beautifully said. She was rather quiet and didn't take suggestive talks or lustful glances lightly. So guys savoured her from a distance with their eyes or their thoughts. A little straight move could easily land one a slap. What she didn't know was that there was a match for her just around the class.

He was Duan and he had a way of getting round to girls' hearts, storming in and more often than not leaving them shattered. Nobody thought he could break into Sinee's heart but he did break into more places than her heart.

Persistence and tact won his day. He lavished her with words that went down in bold to her heart, mind and diary. He made her laugh and damn didn't she look beautiful. It was like a miracle that gave everyone else more reason to try and beat Duan to her heart. Well, for her to wear that smile so permanently in his presence, he must have already been there.

The heart wasn't the only thing she opened up for him. She didn't even know how she ended up giving him so much. She found herself doing it and unable to stop it. Giving him anything he wanted was all she now lived for. Besides, it also made her feel really good. She didn't even know when or how her morals lost grip but they had and it didn't matter as long as she was loosening them up for Duan.

It was just too bad that she got what she didn't bargain for. Duan gave her physical and emotional pleasure. At the same time he also gave her loads of eager semen anxious to procreate. Those loads were quite frequent and often disregarded the concept of safe days. Sinee conceived with only a year to go in high school.

For Duan, it was time to move on and cast his net elsewhere for some fresh catch. That wouldn't be easy. Sinee was too attached and even the school principal knew about the affair. Still Duan wouldn't hang on. His interest was elsewhere. The intensity the storm came with was the same it receded with.

The camera flashed capturing Sinee on film as she lifted up her leg to slip on her panties. She was entirely naked after Duan had just excited pleasure in both of them and filled her up with more foreign bodies in the process.

"What are you doing?" Naive to the brim, she asked. "Just taking myself a souvenir," he promptly answered. "Something to remind me of your sexy body."

She trusted him so much and didn't feel there was anything to trouble her mind. It was okay to believe and trust him but the weekend wasn't over yet.

Monday came and it was back to school. Something strange was happening and for some reason it bothered Sinee. All the boys crowded at a corner looking at something while laughing very loudly. Someone from the crowd even mentioned her name. Before recess, the entire male school community had seen it-the picture of her naked body all courtesy of Duan.

The school administration soon got wind and quickly got hold of the picture. Both their parents were called in and the principal in the presence of the two placed it before them. Sinee could hardly believe that her own father let alone Duan's was looking at her naked self. She stormed out and that marked the end of formal schooling for her.

Hatred for men took a firm grip of her and for

years she didn't entertain any association with them. She just took care of her son Nissa. But her mother was worried. She had booked her exams privately and later took her to college against her husband's will. Now Sinee's years were moving fast and she didn't want her to die alone. So she introduced her to Akkharat who was awed by her looks but not her son. Soon they said the vows and Sinee lived through a marriage filled with fear of being left alone again. Poor Nissa paid the price.

But the angels were there to keep the gate to heaven wide open for an everlasting life. There was nothing of his life to review. He had lived a life too short.

"Welcome to heaven Nissa where there is no pain or sorrow."

10 ALL BUT THE TRUTH

TERROR

What Terror couldn't get rightfully, force always
did the trick. Like everyone else, he wanted to get to
heaven. No angel could keep him out. No one had
ever prevented him from having what he wanted.

"Open the gate," he screamed at the angel. "I'm
sorry I can't."

He got furious. How could someone manning a

gate no matter where it led to deny him entry. Those were the kind of guys he showered with blows and kicks and when his mood was really bad, he'd empty several bullets on their heads.

"Open the gate or I'll make you regret," he ordered. But the angel responded with a smile."

Anger shot up and he jumped onto the gate attempting to scale it.

He slipped back down faster than he went up. He tried again but wouldn't get anywhere near its top to cross over. He tried a third time as he hurled all kinds of abuses at the angel. This time the heavens were fed up.

When his feet came back down, they found no ground to step on. The grounds had opened up and Terror fell through to help build the fires of hell.

ABOUT THE AUTHOR

Joseph Wambua is a teacher by profession. He has a passion for writing especially on topical areas with clear lessons or messages. Lessons combined with entertainment are his style. He has published fiction and educational books for young learners, senior students and adults. Joseph is proudly Kenyan, loves the wild and life at the equator.